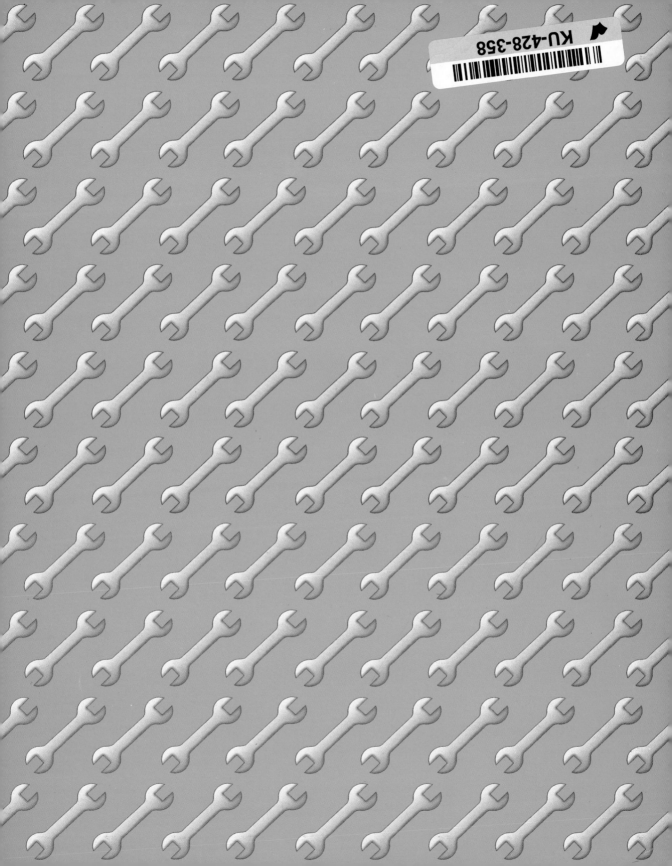

Published by
Armadillo Books
an imprint of
Bookmart Limited
Registered Number 2372865
Trading as Bookmart Limited
Desford Road
Enderby
Leicester
LE9 5AD

ISBN 1-90046-665-1

Produced for
Bookmart Limited by
Nicola Baxter
PO Box 215, Framingham Earl,
Norwich NR14 7UR

Designer: Amanda Hawkes

Printed in Indonesia

Starting to read – no trouble!

The troublesome train in this story helps to make
sharing books at home successful and enjoyable.
The book can be used in several ways to help
beginning readers gain confidence.

You could start by reading the illustrated words
at the edge of each lefthand page with your
child. Have fun trying to spot the same words in
the story itself.

All the words on the righthand pages have already
been met on the facing page. Help your child to
read these by pointing out words and groups of
words already met.

Finally, all the illustrated words can be found
at the end of the book. Enjoy checking all the
words you can both read!

The Trouble with Trains

Written by Nicola Baxter · Illustrated by Geoff Ball

ARMADILLO

train

The new train stands in the station.

Whoo! goes the train.

station

train driver

The train driver is talking to the conductor.

conductor

"What did you say?" asks the conductor.

Whoo! goes the train.

"What did **you** say?" asks the driver.

truck

track

clock

flag

Soon the train is ready to start.

All its trucks are full.

The driver climbs on board.

"We need to go slowly," he says. "There are lots of bends in the track."

Whoo! goes the train.

The driver looks at the station clock.

The conductor waves her flag.

Whoo! The train starts to go.

wheels

cap

trees

fields

"Slowly!" calls the driver.

But the train wants to go faster and faster.

Its wheels rattle along the track.

"Slow down!" calls the driver.
"I almost lost my cap!"

Trees and fields flash past.

"Slow down!" calls the driver.

But the train goes faster and faster.

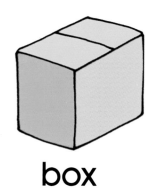

box

bricks

sack

grass

The driver is worried now.

Clunk! A big yellow box falls off a truck.

Crash! Some bricks slip over the side.

Thud! A sack of potatoes bounces on the grass. The potatoes roll everywhere.

"What are you doing?" cries the driver.

Still the train does not slow down.

hill

Whoo! The train rattles up a hill.

More boxes fall off.

bridge

Whoo! The train rattles over a bridge. More bricks are lost.

tunnel

signal

Whoo! The train goes through a tunnel.

"Slow down!" shouts the driver. "There's a signal ahead!"

The train goes through the signal!

watch

Luckily, the signal is green.

Up ahead is the next station.
The train slows down at last.

drink

biscuit

The driver looks at his watch
and shakes his head.

"I need a cold drink and a
biscuit," he says.

workman

A workman comes to unload
the train.

The workman shakes his head.

glass

plate

"That's funny," he says. "The boxes and bricks and sacks are gone! Oh no! I'm in trouble."

bench

The driver puts down his glass and his plate. He gets up from his bench.

"We'll go back as quickly as we can," he says, "for more boxes and bricks and potatoes."

potatoes

Whoo! The train can't wait to go fast again.

That's the trouble with trains!

Picture dictionary

Now you can read these words!

bench

biscuit

box

bricks

bridge

cap

clock

conductor

drink

fields

flag

glass

grass

hill

plate

potatoes

sack

signal

station

track

train driver

trees

truck

tunnel

watch

wheels

workman

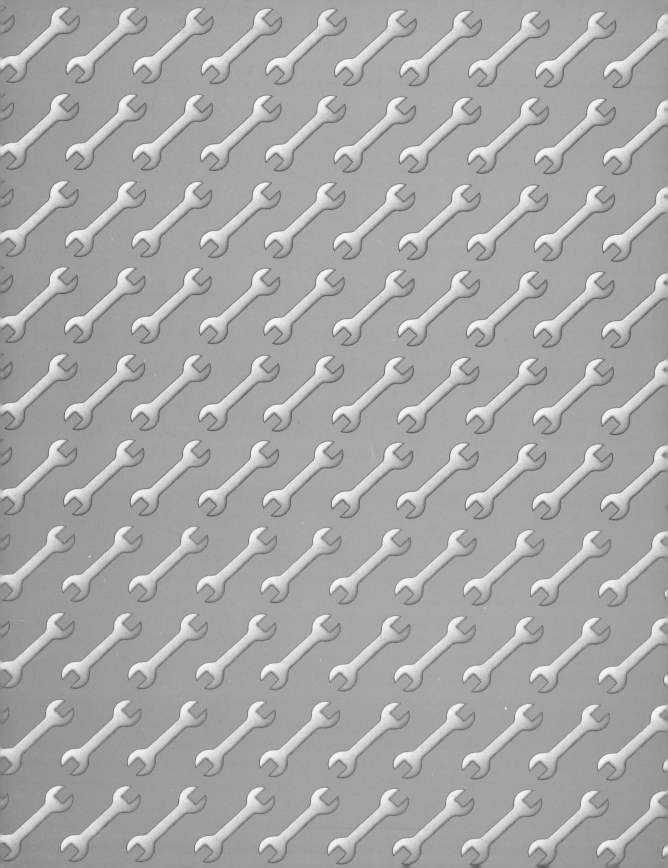